FOR LARA - A. W.

FOR MIKE & MARIE - D. B.

tiger tales
5 River Road, Suite 128, Wilton, CT 06897
Published in the United States 2021
Originally published in Great Britain 2021
by Little Tiger Press Ltd.

Text copyright © 2021 Angela Woolfe
Illustrations copyright © 2021 Duncan Beedie
ISBN-13: 978-1-68010-257-4
ISBN-10: 1-68010-257-5

Printed in China • LTP/2800/3721/0221
All rights reserved • 10 9 8 7 6 5 4 3 2 1

www.tigertalesbooks.com

AGENT LLAMA

BY

ANGELA WOOLFE

ILLUSTRATED BY

DUNCAN BEEDIE

tiger tales

A mountainside; a snowy slope —
a **SPY** looks through a telescope.

She slaloms down the hill with ease
on double pairs of *JET-BLACK* skis,

then fires a dart
to fell a
GOON.

Just a normal afternoon for
CHARLIE PALMER, super spy—
this llama ALWAYS
gets her guy.

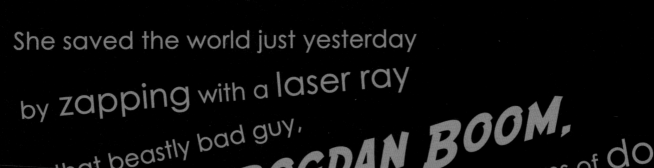

She saved the world just yesterday by zapping with a laser ray that beastly bad guy, *BOGDAN BOOM,* a scientist with dreams of doom.

Boom, Bogdan

...r-Duper Laser Blaster (Mk. I)

Target Profile:

BOOM 72350

Name: Bogdan Boom

Species: Musk Ox

Height: 3' 6"

Weight: Unknown

Favorite food: Smoky bacon chips

Characteristics: Short stature, very grumpy.

Mission Objective: Capture Boom and disable super-duper laser blaster.

Mission Status: INCOMPLETE

BOOM ESCAPES!

Right now, she's on another case — the reason for the high-speed chase —

INCOMING CALL: HQ

a **CALL** is coming through from Charlie's boss at Spy HQ.

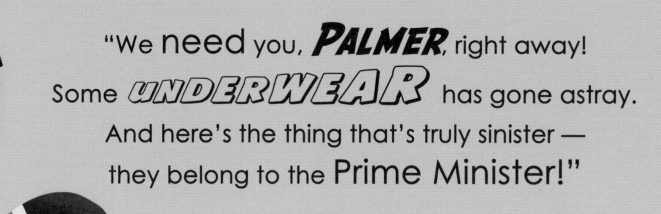

"We need you, **PALMER**, right away!
Some *UNDERWEAR* has gone astray.
And here's the thing that's truly sinister —
they belong to the Prime Minister!"

BREAKING: PM'S UNDIES GO A.W.O.L.   BRIEFING ON BRIEFS TO FOLLOW...

THE LLAMA CAN'T BELIEVE THE NEWS:

"It's not a **THEFT** that I would choose,

but do not **PANIC** or **DESPAIR**—

I'll find that missing underwear!"

Two hours later, here she is: onboard a plane with lemon fizz.
Her brand-new gadgets lie about:

STINK BOMB in a Brussels sprout;
bag of chips (with **JET PROPELLER**);

parachute (in small umbrella);
SPORTS CAR in a ping-pong ball.

YIKES!

The plane begins to fall!

Charlie races up to see:
"The pilot's gone! It's only me!"

She takes control and starts to climb;
a mountain looms . . . she's **just** in time!

The fuel light's flashing! **Hotshot** llamas don't do crashing!

A SPRINT,

A JUMP . . .

a **PERFECT** landing!

(This llama, guys . . . she's just outstanding.)

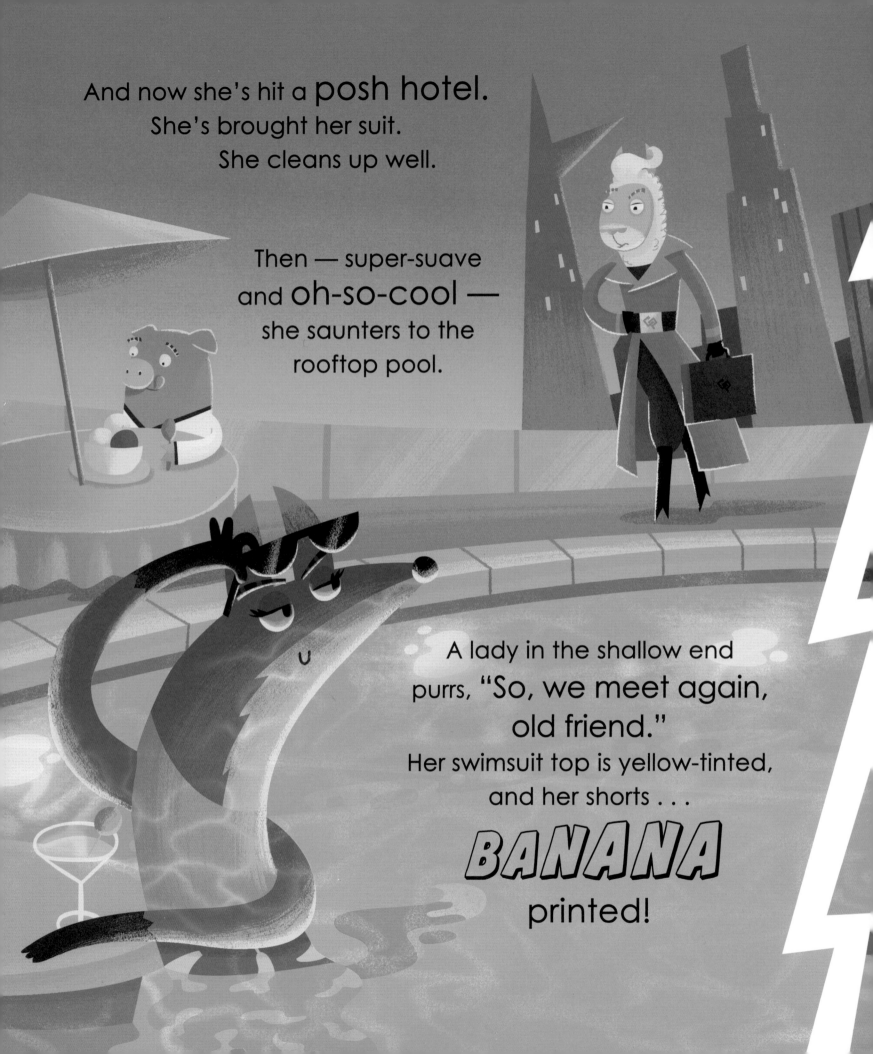

And now she's hit a posh hotel.
She's brought her suit.
She cleans up well.

Then — super-suave
and oh-so-cool —
she saunters to the
rooftop pool.

A lady in the shallow end
purrs, "So, we meet again,
old friend."
Her swimsuit top is yellow-tinted,
and her shorts . . .
BANANA
printed!

"**GRETA GRIMM,** so you're involved!
The undies-theft has now been solved.

So hand them back — **IT'S OVER,** Grimm!"
But Greta just resumes her swim.
Her **GOONS** are coming — there are SIX!

KUNG

FU

KICKS!

Grimm sobs, "You won! I feel so silly.
Help me out! I'm getting chilly."

Our **heroine** extends a hoof
(her swanky suit is waterproof)
and takes Grimm's hand, but . . .

ZING!

She's zapped!

TRAPDOOR

The pool floor opens,

and now she's

TRAPPED!

Charlie wakes up inside a **lair**. She's tied tightly to a chair,

Super Duper Laser Blaser Mk. II

TO-DO LIST:
Get quote for lunar base
Crush henchmen's union
Buy shark repellent
Check handcuffs (again!)
Knit pair of socks

and watching her from across the room are **GRETA GRIMM** and **BOGDAN BOOM.**

"Our trap has worked!
We've lured her in!"
shrieks Bogdan Boom.
"At last, I win!

This llama spy has
laughed her last!
So long, old girl —
it's been a BLAST."

An evil grin contorts his face:
"Give my regards to

OUTER
SPACE!"

She must escape! She **MUST!**

Our **hero** is in quite a fix!
She needs her case of techno tricks.

"I'm beaten, Boom, and you're the winner. Won't you grant me one last dinner?

A **BRUSSELS SPROUT**, a **CHIP** or two. I'll even share the **BAG** with you!"

"Ooh, chips," says **BOOM**. "Untie her, Greta. Smoky bacon? Even better!"

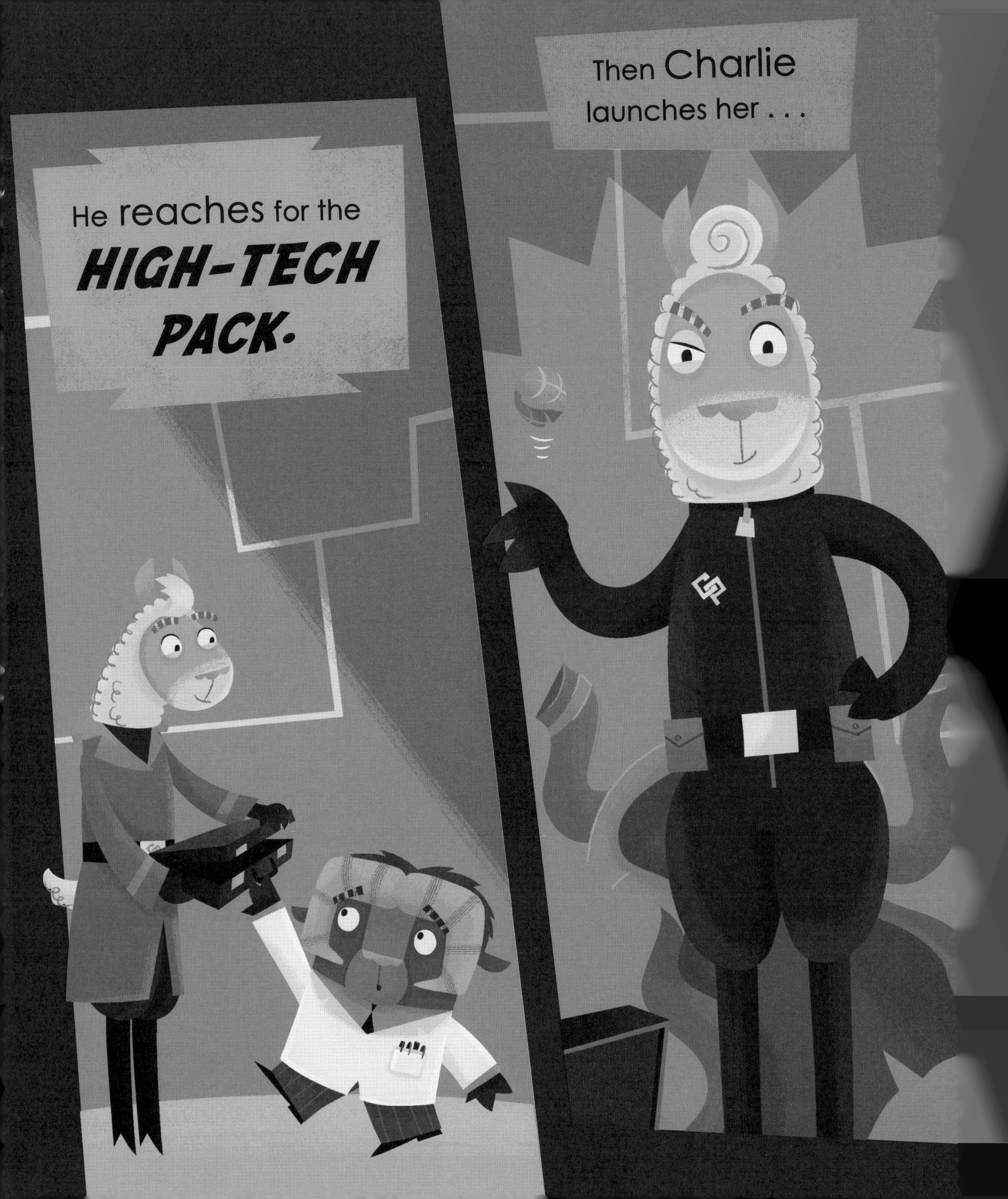
He reaches for the HIGH-TECH PACK.
Then Charlie launches her . . .

ATTACK!

She chucks a **sprout**; it hits the floor,
and smelly smoke
begins to pour.

"It stinks!" screams Boom,
who cannot see.

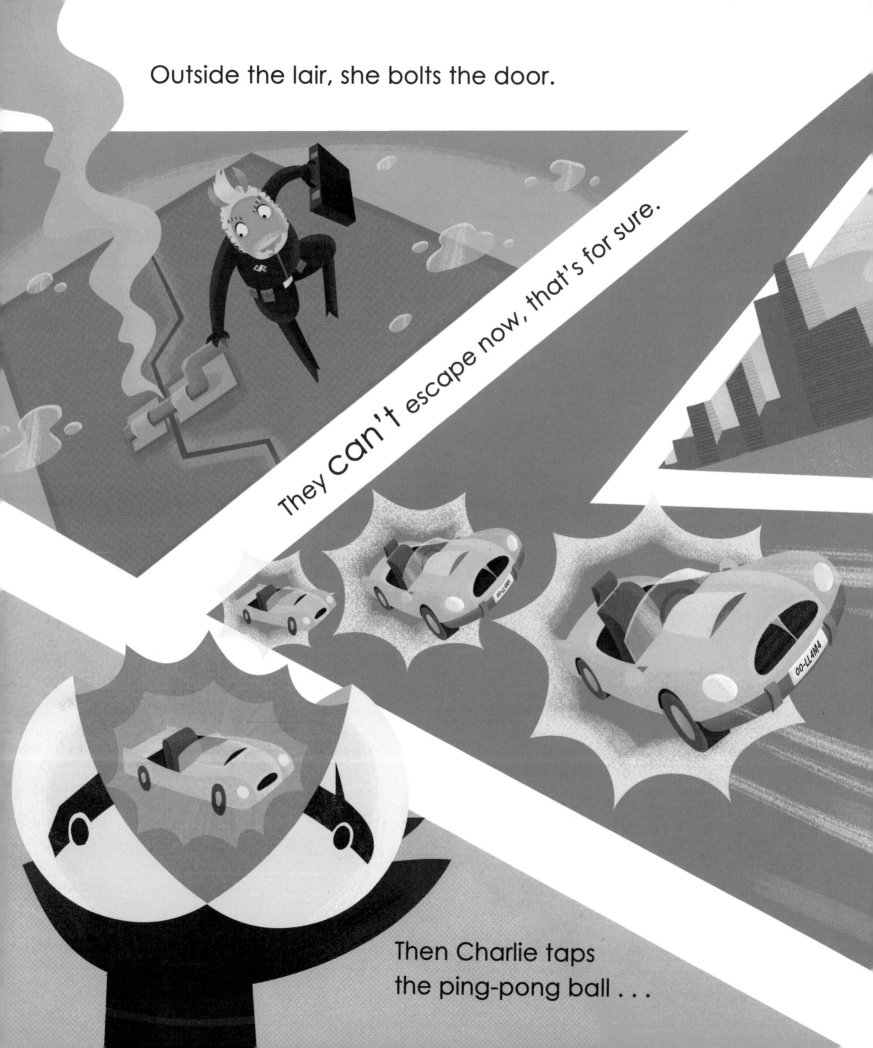

Outside the lair, she bolts the door.

They can't escape now, that's for sure.

Then Charlie taps
the ping-pong ball . . .

. . . and from her car, she makes a call:

HQ? SUCCESS!
WE'VE SAVED THE NATION.
I THINK I'VE EARNED A
SHORT VACATION.

COAST

The car

ZOOMS off,

and soon she'll reach . . .